A Note to Parents

For many children, learning math is difficult and "I hate math!" is their first response — to which many parents silently add "Me, too!" Children often see adults comfortably reading and writing, but they rarely have such models for mathematics. And math fear can be catching!

The easy-to-read stories in this **Hello Math** series were written to give children a positive introduction to mathematics and parents a pleasurable re-acquaintance with a subject that is important to everyone's life. **Hello Math** stories make mathematical ideas accessible, interesting, and fun for children. The activities and suggestions at the end of each book provide parents with a hands-on approach to helping children develop mathematical interest and confidence.

Enjoy the mathematics!

• Give your child a chance to retell the story. The more familiar children are with the story, the more they will understand its mathematical concepts.

• Use the colorful illustrations to help children "hear and see" the math at work in the story.

• Treat the math activities as games to be played for fun. Follow your child's lead. Spend time on those activities that engage your child's interest and curiosity.

• Activities, especially ones using physical materials, help make abstract mathematical ideas concrete.

Learning is a messy process and learning about math calls for children to become immersed in lively experiences that help them make sense of mathematical concepts and symbols.

Although learning about numbers is basic to math, other ideas, such as identifying shapes and patterns, measuring, collecting and interpreting data, reasoning logically, and thinking about chance are also important. By reading these stories and having fun with the activities, you'll help your child enthusiastically say "**Hello, Math,**" instead of "I hate math."

—Marilyn Burns
National Mathematics Educator
Author of *The I Hate Mathematics! Book*

For K.D., the happiest ending
— S.K.

For Wes
— H.H.

Text and art copyright © 1996 by Scholastic Inc.
The activities on pages 27-32 copyright © 1996 by Marilyn Burns.
All rights reserved. Published by Scholastic Inc.
HELLO READER!, CARTWHEEL BOOKS, and the CARTWHEEL BOOKS logo are registered trademarks of Scholastic Inc.

Library of Congress Cataloging-in-Publication Data
Keenan, Sheila.
    The biggest fish / by Sheila Keenan ; illustrated by Holly Hannon.
    p. cm. — (Hello math reader. Level 3)
    "Cartwheel Books."
    Summary: The mayor's contest to find the biggest fish in Littletown is won in an unexpected way.
    ISBN 0-590-26600-4
    [1. Fishing — Fiction. 2. Fishes — Fiction. 3. Contests — Fiction.] I. Hannon, Holly, ill. II. Title. III. Series.
    PZ7.K2295Bi 1996
    [E] — dc20   95-13240
                                                              CIP
                                                               AC

16 15 14 13 12   34/0

Printed in the U.S.A.   23

First Scholastic printing, February 1996

THE BIGGEST FISH

by Sheila Keenan
Illustrated by Holly Hannon

Hello Math Reader — Level 3

SCHOLASTIC INC.
Cartwheel B·O·O·K·S·®

New York Toronto London Auckland Sydney

The mayor of Littletown
was not happy.
Other towns had big houses.
Other towns had big stores.
Other towns even had big vegetables!

"Littletown needs something big!"
the mayor said.

He had an idea.
He put up a sign.
Everybody in Littletown read it.

People ran this way with fishing poles
and that way with fishing nets.

The mayor sat in a big chair.
He waited.

The baker was first in line.
"I've got it!" he cried.
"I caught a fish as big as
five fat loaves of bread!"

"That's a big fish," said the mayor.
He made a note.

"Wait!" someone yelled.

"Look here," said the farmer.
He was second in line.
"My fish is as tall
as my corn is high."

"Maybe that's a bigger fish, all right,"
the mayor said.
He wrote in the farmer's name.

"Hold it!" came a voice.

The mayor knew that voice.

It was his wife! She stood
third in line.

"I caught a fish as big as
our couch," she said.
"Here is a picture of it, dear."

"Yes, this is the biggest fish,"
the mayor agreed.

He put his wife's name at the top of his list.

HONK! HONK! HONK!

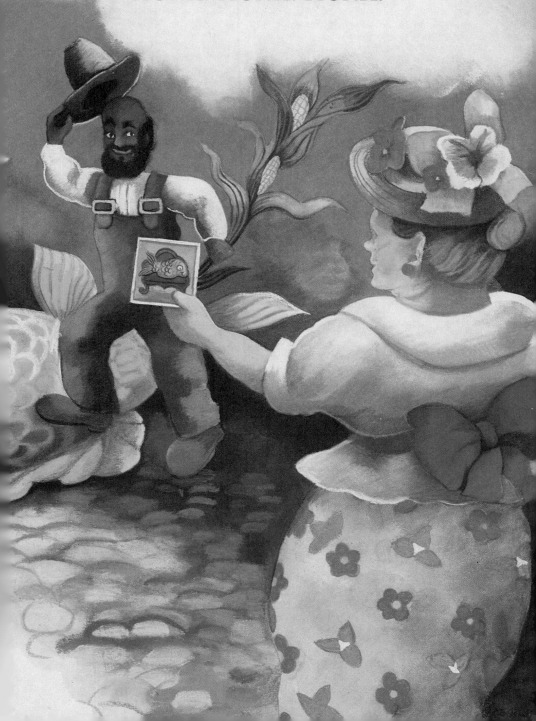

A bus rolled into the fourth
place in line.

"Check out my fish,"
the bus driver said.
"This fish is so heavy
I had to drive it here."

The mayor looked at the bus.
A fish tail stuck out of
the back door.

"Could this be the very biggest fish?"
he said.

"Whoa!" someone called.

It was the zookeeper.
She was fifth in line.
Her two sisters were with her.

"Look at this huge snake.

Now look at this huge fish.
It's a winner!" the zookeeper said.

"This is surely the very, very biggest fish!" said the mayor.

"I don't think so," someone cried.

The firefighter dragged
his hose,
a fish,
and himself
into the sixth place in line.

"Which is longer, a snake
or a fire hose?" he asked.

"Hmmm," said the mayor.

"Right!" said the firefighter.
"*My* hose—and *my* fish!"

"Then this is the biggest of big fish,"
the mayor said.

"Maybe yes, maybe no,"
came a voice.

Everyone turned around.
Last in line was a painter.

"Well?" said the mayor.
"I have a fish," said the painter.

"My fish is as big as a building.
It's a whole block long.
My fish is too heavy to bring here!"

"Impossible!" cried the firefighter.
"Impossible!" cried the zookeeper.
"Impossible!" cried the bus driver.
"Impossible!" cried the mayor's wife,
the farmer, and the baker.

"Indeed!" said the mayor. "Let's see
this very biggest of very big fish."

"Come with me," said the painter.

So they all followed the painter. . . .

"Here it is!" the painter said.
The townspeople gasped.

"This isn't a real fish!"
cried the zookeeper.
Everyone nodded.

"The mayor's sign did not say
a *real* fish," said the painter.
"It said the *biggest* fish!"

"That fish is the longest,"
said the mayor. "It's the tallest.
It's the fattest. It's the heaviest."

"So it *is* the biggest fish,"
the mayor's wife added.

"And it's given me a BIG idea!"
the mayor shouted.
"We have a winner!"

"Do you have any more paint?"

The next day there was finally
something big in Littletown.

• ABOUT THE ACTIVITIES •

Measurement is an important and practical part of mathematics. We measure the temperature outside, the length of the hallway to see if a rug will fit, a cup of flour for a recipe, the air pressure in our automobile tires. We've learned to use standard units to communicate about the sizes of things, letting the purpose of our measuring determine how accurate we need to be.

Young children are naturally interested in the sizes of things, and comparing objects is their first measuring experience. Children often start with whether things are big or little. Further sorting and comparing helps them become aware of the specific physical properties of objects. They begin to use more precise vocabulary: longer or shorter, heavier or lighter, thicker or thinner, taller or shorter, and so on.

When children can't compare two objects directly, they find some go-between to help them measure — sticks, handspans, footsteps, blocks, or whatever they have at hand. Measurement tools like these, though nonstandard and imprecise, lay the foundation for children's later learning about using standard measures and being more accurate.

The activities and games in this section give children firsthand experiences with measuring in different ways. The directions are written for you to read along with your child. Follow your child's interests, and enjoy measuring with your child!

— Marilyn Burns

You'll find tips and suggestions
for guiding the activities whenever
you see a box like this!

Order, Please!

The firefighter says his hose is longer than the zookeeper's snake. How could you find out if this is true? See if this activity gives you any ideas.

Find five to ten things. Compare which are longer and which are shorter. You can use cut strips of paper, or find things in the house like pencils, straws, or lengths of ribbon or string to compare. Now line them up in size order.

> You may want to start with just three objects. If your child can order them and is interested in more, then let your child add others.

Out of Sight

Try this measuring game for two people. You'll need a ball of string and a pair of scissors.

Decide on something to measure: the length of a fork, around a jar, or across a book. Both of you look at the object until you're ready to measure it.

Once you're both ready, put the object out of sight. Then each of you cuts a piece of string that you think is just the right length. Then take the object and see how you did. Who got closer?

Try the game with other objects.

Try this: Take two identical straws, pens, or pencils or cut two identical strips of paper. Place them side by side. Most likely, your child will agree that one is as long as the other. Then slide one down a bit. Ask your child if they're still the same length. Don't be surprised if your child insists that one is longer! Young children typically connect measurement with position, but with time and more experiences, children's understanding develops. Encourage your child to match objects to compare them.

Step Counts

People in the story used things around them to measure. You can use your own two feet to do this at home.

Decide on at least three different distances to measure, like:
from your bed to your bedroom door;
from the kitchen to the living room;
from the front door to your bedroom door.

Guess how many footsteps it will take you to go each distance. You may want to write down your guess. Then try it and see.

If your mom or dad did the same, do you think she or he would need more steps or fewer steps? Guess and then count. What did you learn?

This game gives your child experience estimating distances and then measuring to check. Remember, the goal is not to estimate correctly, but for the child to compare the predictions with the actual count.

Measuring Tools

What tools might have helped the mayor measure the fish? See which of these measuring tools you have in your house or at school: ruler, yardstick, tape measure, measuring cup, measuring spoons, scales, thermometers, calendar. For each one, think of the kinds of things you can measure with it.

Do you know about any other measuring tools?

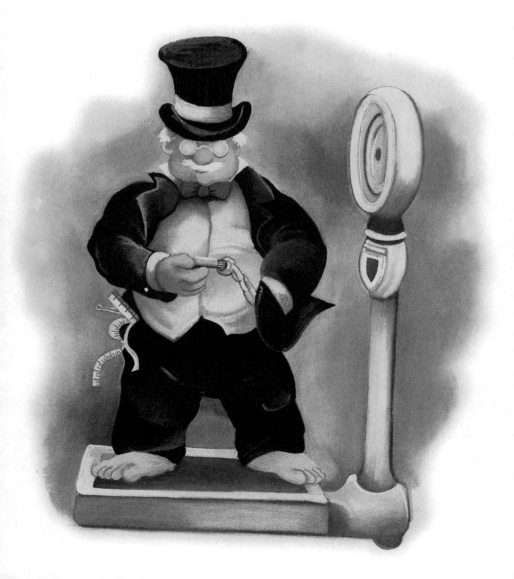

Dot Dot

This measuring game can be tricky. You'll need two pieces of paper that are exactly the same size and shape. Put a dot on one of them, anywhere you want. Leave that paper and go into another room; bring a pencil and the unmarked paper.

Now your job is to put the same size dot on the second piece of paper in exactly the same spot! The tricky part is that the two papers are in different rooms. You can go back to look at the first paper, but you can't take it out of the room. You have to figure out some other way to draw the second dot! When you think you have it, hold your papers together and compare dots.

Children may choose to use a ruler, measure with their hands, or try some other method. Let them experiment!